Raise Your Hand if This is You

EXPLORING CHILDREN'S
DIFFERENCES AND
UNDERSTANDING NEEDS

By B. G. BAKER
ILLUSTRATED BY: JEANNINE CORCORAN

Raise Your Hand if This is You
Copyright © 2022 by B. G. Baker

All rights reserved. No part of this publication may be reproduced, distributed, or transmitted in any form or by any means, including photocopying, recording, or other electronic or mechanical methods, without the prior written permission of the author, except in the case of brief quotations embodied in critical reviews and certain other non-commercial uses permitted by copyright law.

Tellwell Talent
www.tellwell.ca

ISBN
978-0-2288-8242-8 (Hardcover)
978-0-2288-8240-4 (Paperback)
978-0-2288-8241-1 (eBook)

Author's Note

I was inspired to write this book when my daughter noticed children staring at her because she does not have hair. At age four, she permanently lost her hair from radiation treatments to her brain to fight a brain tumor, Pineoblastoma. She would bury her face in my side when children would stare. I explained that they only stare because they want to understand why you do not have hair. They wouldn't stare if they knew why. This book was written to encourage children to ask questions and to nurture their curiosity. Each page is an opportunity for parents, educators, and caregivers to discuss our special differences and to understand we all have needs. I want to thank my sister the teacher, Shelia, for her encouragement and support in making this book happen. Thank you, Carolina, for your help in making all of my pieces fit. Thank you to the women that have molded me Mom, Granny, Aunt Sandy, Aunt Barbara, Aunt Marlene, and Darla. To my boys, Chris, Jonathan, Bailey, and Chase, I love you! I would not be where I am today without my rock, Justin. To you, the reader, stay curious and kind my friend.

For Nova
"No hair, don't care"

We are all special, and we all have needs.
When you put the two words together,
what do they mean?
Special can be better or unlike the usual.
Your needs can be required or crucial.
What makes you special from others?
Maybe you have no sisters, only brothers.

Do you wear glasses?

Are you allergic to cheese or molasses?

Do you walk or push cool wheels? Maybe you're clumsy and slip on banana peels.

Do you read with your hands?

Do you play an instrument in a band?

Can you talk with your fingers?

Are you in a choir singing with singers?

Are you smaller than the rest?

Can you color the best?

Do you see letters on paper different from how they sound?

Is your sense of smell as strong as a hound?

Does your laugh sound like a heckle?

Do you have cute little freckles?

Does your smile have a dimple?

Do you make dancing look simple?

We are all unique as the veins in the leaves; now, let's talk about our "Special Needs."

Do you need help when you are lost?

Can you twist open your applesauce?

Is your food fed through a tube?

Do you have an animal that helps to change your mood?

Do you have a device in your ear to help you hear?

Do you wear a particular pair of glasses that help colors appear?

EMERGENCY NUMBERS

Mom's number:
123-555-1111

Dad's number:
123-222-4444

Dede and Memaw:
123-333-8888

For emergencies:
911

What if there were an emergency? Do you know how to call your mommy or daddy?

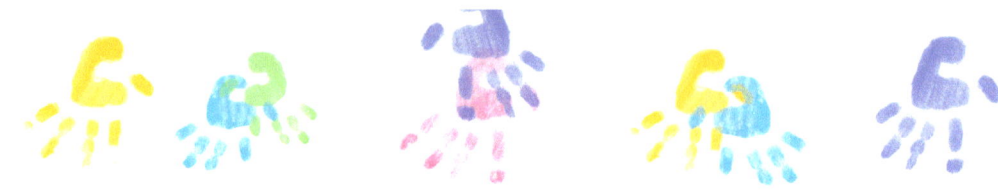

Can you drive to school all by yourself?

Can you pull up your socks?

What about poking your straw through your juice box?

Are there training wheels on your bike?

Can you go all by yourself on a mountain hike?

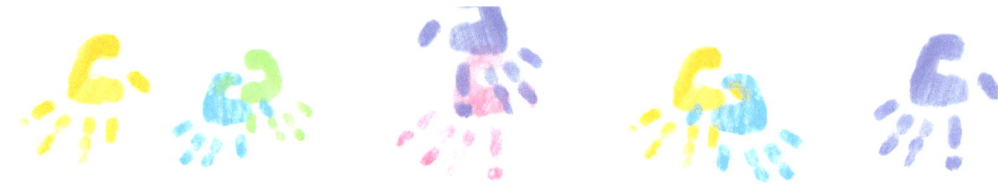

Whatever your need and whatever your uniqueness may be, we all need a little help, you see.

Printed in the USA
CPSIA information can be obtained
at www.ICGtesting.com
LVHW072235220823
756013LV00012B/33